Thoth: The History and Legacy of the Ancient Egyptian God Who Maintains the Universe

By Markus Carabas and Charles River Editors

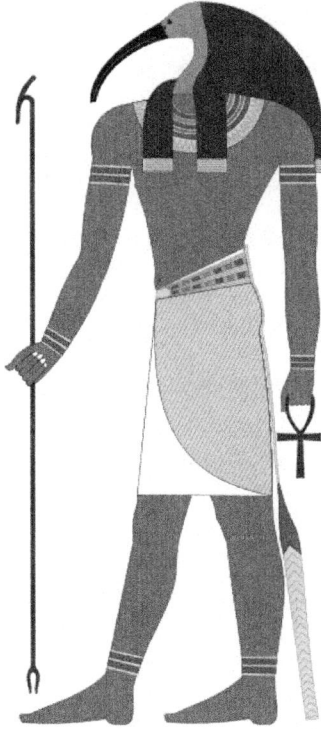

Jeff Dahl's depiction of Thoth

About Charles River Editors

Charles River Editors is a boutique digital publishing company, specializing in bringing history back to life with educational and engaging books on a wide range of topics. Keep up to date with our new and free offerings with this 5 second sign up on our weekly mailing list, and visit Our Kindle Author Page to see other recently published Kindle titles.

We make these books for you and always want to know our readers' opinions, so we encourage you to leave reviews and look forward to publishing new and exciting titles each week.

Introduction

Thoout, Thoth Deux fois Grand, le Second Hermés

Thoth

"Thus says Thoth, judge of truth, to the Great Ennead which is in the presence of Osiris: Hear this word of very truth. I have judged the heart of the deceased and his soul stands as a witness for him. His deeds are righteous in the great balance, and no sin has been found in him…"[1]

Africa may have given rise to the first human beings, and Egypt probably gave rise to the first great civilizations, which continue to fascinate modern societies across the globe nearly 5,000 years later. From the Library and Lighthouse of Alexandria to the Great Pyramid at Giza, the Ancient Egyptians produced several wonders of the world, revolutionized architecture and construction, created some of the world's first systems of mathematics and medicine, and established language and art that spread across the known world. With world-famous leaders like King Tut and Cleopatra, it's no wonder that today's world has so many Egyptologists.

---

[1] Spell 30b *Book of the Dead*, trans. Faulkner 2001

What makes the accomplishments of the Ancient Egyptians all the more remarkable is that Egypt was historically a place of great political turbulence. Its position made it both valuable and vulnerable to tribes across the Mediterranean and the Middle East, and Ancient Egypt had no shortage of its own internecine warfare. Its most famous conquerors would come from Europe, with Alexander the Great laying the groundwork for the Hellenic Ptolemy line and the Romans extinguishing that line after defeating Cleopatra and driving her to suicide.

Perhaps the most intriguing aspect of ancient Egyptian civilization was its inception from the ground up, as the ancient Egyptians had no prior civilization which they could use as a template. In fact, ancient Egypt itself became a template for the civilizations that followed. The Greeks and the Romans were so impressed with Egyptian culture that they often attributed many attributes of their own culture–usually erroneously–to the Egyptians. With that said, some minor elements of ancient Egyptian culture were, indeed, passed on to later civilizations. Egyptian statuary appears to have had an initial influence on the Greek version, and the ancient Egyptian language continued long after the pharaonic period in the form of the Coptic language.

Although the Egyptians may not have passed their civilization directly on to later peoples, the key elements that comprised Egyptian civilization, including their religion, early ideas of state, and art and architecture, can be found among other civilizations. For instance, civilizations far separated in time and space, such as China and Mesoamerica, possessed key elements that were similar to those found in ancient Egypt. Indeed, since Egyptian civilization represented some fundamental human concepts, a study of their culture can be useful when trying to understand many other pre-modern cultures.

To the ancient Egyptians, as was the case with any society made up of inquiring humans, the world was a confusing and often terrifying place of destruction, death and unexplained phenomena. In order to make sense of such an existence, they resorted to teleological stories. Giving a phenomenon a story made it less horrifying, and it also helped them make sense of the world around them. Unsurprisingly, then, the ancient Egyptian gods permeated every aspect of existence.

Baboons held a prestigious place in Egyptian religion. They were kept as sacred animals in many temples because contemporary Egyptians considered them the original religious observers, particularly with respect to the sun god Re. Ancient Egyptians took the wild baboons stretching on their hind legs, forelegs raised to the sky, to be an oration to the sun god at dawn. Furthermore, these ancient ancestors of the land of Egypt were greeted at dawn by the concatenations of the baboons nattering, which the religious-minded took to be an early-morning devotion and even believed that the baboons spoke the original language of religion, and a claim they could understand baboons was often one asserted by certain members of the priestly class.

However, it is his association with the ibis that most defines Thoth's visual imagery. Since the ancient Egyptians believed that the universe arose from the swamp-like waters of Nun, it was the water bird that garnered the most prestigious veneration. Birds like geese, herons and the ibises were associated with this period of creation, and, according to some beliefs, the world came about thanks to the great "honk" of a primordial goose, whose eggshell was said to be preserved in the temple of Thoth. It was believed that Re created Thoth's baboon form to be that of his "shining moon," but his ibis form was that of a messenger between heaven and earth (although he was much more than this).

Thoth: The History and Legacy of the Ancient Egyptian God Who Maintains the Universe looks at the mythology surrounding one of antiquity's most famous deities. Along with pictures depicting important people, places, and events, you will learn about Thoth like never before.

Note

The absolute dating of individual pharaohs has been a matter of long debate among Egyptologists, mostly due to the existence of several king lists that vary in the number of years they assign to each ruler.

The basic outline comes from Manetho, one of two priestly advisors to Ptolemy I (305-282 BCE). Manetho's *History* divides the pharaohs into 30 native dynasties and gives the number of years each ruler was on the throne, but no complete copy of Manetho's work exists.

Other king lists are also fragmentary. The Palermo Stone from Dynasty V (2498-2345 BCE) is a fairly complete list starting from the last Predynastic kings, but it sadly ends in the middle of Dynasty V. The Royal List of Karnak goes all the way to Tuthmosis III (1504-1450 BCE) and is especially useful in that it records many of the minor rulers of the Second Intermediate Period, when Egypt was divided into two or more states. The Royal List of Abydos skips these kings but runs all the way to the reign of Seti I (1291-1278 BCE). The Royal Canon of Turin is a badly damaged papyrus dating to around 1200 BCE that gives the precise length of reign of each ruler, often down to the day. Many portions of the list are missing, however.

Discoveries of other texts and radiocarbon dating have helped refine the dates, but there are still competing theories regarding the chronology, and all have both merits and problems. For the sake of consistency, this work uses the chronology set forth by Egyptologist Peter A. Clayton in his various works. The reader should note that while Clayton's chronology is a popular one, it is by no means universally accepted.

The Origins of Ancient Egyptian Mythology

Ancient Egypt spans a history of some 3,000 years, depending on how people want to divide it up. Many cultures, such as ancient Greece, divided their lengthy histories either according to cultural changes, such as the "Classical Era" beginning with the onset of democracy and ending with the death of Alexander the Great, or by following the reigns of each subsequent ruler. In ancient Egypt, the vast history was originally divided into dynasties. Living in the 3rd century BCE, the Egyptian priest Manetho divided history into 30 dynasties, which later Egyptologists have grouped into longer periods according to how much of what is considered Egypt today fell under the rule of each king. They are given as follows, according to Shaw's chronology:[2]

The Pharaonic Period

Early Dynastic Period (Dynasties 1-2) ca.3050-2660 BCE

Old Kingdom (Dynasties 3-6) ca. 2660-2190 BCE

---

[2] Shaw 2015

First Intermediate Period (Dynasties 7-11) ca. 2190-2066 BCE

Middle Kingdom (Dynasties 11-12) ca. 2066-1780 BCE

Second Intermediate Period (Dynasties 13-17) ca. 1780-1549 BCE

New Kingdom (Dynasties 18-20) ca. 1549-1069 BCE

Third Intermediate Period (21-25) ca. 1069-664 BCE

Late Period (Dynasties 26-31) ca. 664-332 BCE

The Ptolemaic Period 332-30 BCE

The Roman Period 30 BCE – 395 CE

In order to understand why modern scholars chose to divide history into longer periods of dynastic rule, it is necessary to understand the geography of Egypt's ruled dominions. The river that defined and dictated much of ancient people's lives and ideologies, the Nile, runs from south to north, with a sprawling delta in the north and more barren land to the south. This distinction is the reason for one of the most confusing aspects of Egyptian history, as the "Upper Kingdom" was in the south and the "Lower Kingdom" was in the north.[3] These "Two Lands" were represented by two distinct crowns – the "Red Crown" for the Lower Kingdom and the "White Crown" for the "Upper Kingdom" – each worn by their distinct rulers and worn as a "Double Crown" when both kingdoms were unified. It was during the "intermediate" periods that the country was divided into the two kingdoms, and these periods were often marked by political turmoil and a distinct drop in cultural production, such as art and architecture.

From as early as the Early Dynastic Period, the country was divided into smaller dominions along the river that modern scholars call "Nomes". The word "nome" comes from the ancient Greeks who, during the rule of the Greek Ptolemaic dynasty (332-30 BCE) in Egypt, referred to each as a kind of "pasturage" coming under the overarching rule of the Pharaoh of that kingdom. This made for a useful way of organising the inhabitants of the two kingdoms, but it causes problems when trying to define what version of a common myth is the "correct" or "most widely believed". The reason for this is that the myths, though they had some similarities, could diverge widely from nome to nome. That is why writers such as the ancient historian Plutarch chose to single out a particular version of a myth and record or study it alone.

Later scholars further subdivided these various types of myth according to the cult center that either produced or 'standardized" them.[4] They refer to them as "theologies," such as the "Memphite Theology" (myths from Memphis) or the "Heliopolitan Theology" (myths from

---

[3] Shaw 2015
[4] Shaw 2015

Heliopolis). There is the theory that these "theologies" were competing in some way with others from different cult centers. Shaw, however, takes the view that they were more alternatives than opposing theories and although each cult center would substitute a god from another nome for one of their own local deities, there wasn't really any kind of animosity between the differing believers. Despite the fact that there was no externally enforced dogma over the whole of Egypt, the Egyptians still managed to maintain some overarching concepts. One such concept is that of the creation of the universe. Generally speaking, there was a limitless dark ocean of "chaos" called Nun, out of which a god was born who instigated creation.[5] The different cult centers felt at liberty to amend or augment that concept to incorporate local tastes and allegiances to deities. Later on, during the period of the New Kingdom, the cult center of Thebes gained prominence and the priests there tried to unify the earlier traditions of Egypt. In this attempt, Amun was the creator god but the Thebans also incorporated the traditions of the major cult centers like Hermopolis, Memphis and Heliopolis, which often seem quite disparate accounts to the modern reader but were quite ingeniously brought together at Thebes around 1200 BCE.[6]

The general creation story contains within it two aspects that are crucial to understanding all of the myths of ancient Egypt: *maat* and *isfet*. Isfet represents chaos or disorder, generally speaking, and it was seen as a fundamental element of everything in existence. There was no notion of trying to eradicate isfet from their general lives in ancient Egypt; after all, it was said to be one of the elements that was present in the limitless ocean at the dawn of creation. The only desire for ancient Egyptians was that isfet never became more prevalent than maat, its opposite: justice. Maat was often depicted as a goddess wearing a feather on her head, which was also the hieroglyph that represented her.[7] She, or simply the concept of justice, was believed to be present in all aspects of life and if it was broken by anyone, there would be a punishment. According to the Middle Kingdom "Coffin Text" it was believed that Atum, the "Great Finisher" of creation,[8] inhaled maat in order to gain his consciousness: "Inhale your daughter Maat [said Nun to Atum] and raise her to your nostril so that your consciousness may live. May they not be far from you, your daughter Maat and your son Shu, whose name is "life" … it is your son Shu who will lift you up."[9]

After that, Atum was capable of making the waters of Nun recede away from him, making him rise above them and become "what remained" or the "mound of creation." It's important to take note of the fact that there was no creation until Atum inhaled life and justice. Therefore without maat and her dualistic counterpart, there would have been no world, and that is the reason for maat and isfet's ubiquity, as well as the acceptance of chaos in the world as seen by the ancient Egyptians. After Atum had separated himself from Nun, the children he kept inside, notably Shu

[5] Shaw 2015
[6] Shaw 2015
[7] Shaw 2015
[8] Shaw 2015
[9] 80 see Shaw 2015

and maat/isfet, often represented as a form of the goddess Tefnut, were now separated from their father, and Tefnut would go on to become the mother of all the gods.

The Recording of The Myths

Since each of the nomes had their own version of a given myth, collecting Egyptian myths into a definitive text was never possible. This has further exacerbated the mythologist's job, since these stories have survived in disparate versions and media.

The myths may have arrived at the hands of scholars from inscriptions on pyramid walls (such as the Old Kingdom's "Pyramid Texts"), painted on the inside of coffins (such as the Middle Kingdom's "Coffin Texts"), or texts written on papyri (such as the famous "Book of the Dead," which dates back to the Second Intermediate Period).[10] The mythologist's job is made even more exacting by the fact that, since the scribes who documented the myths assumed their readers were knowledgeable about the stories" details, they opted to refer to myths obliquely out of a sense of decorum. This was often the case for Osiris, whose death was a troublesome topic for those inscribing on the funerary monuments since it was thought that simply mentioning his death could "magically harm the deceased."[11]

---

[10] Shaw 2015
[11] Shaw 2015

Scenes from the Book of the Dead

The vast history of Egypt makes tracking the development of certain myths a complex process. In terms of the oldest description of death, modern scholars have the Pyramid Texts. These were initially inscribed on the walls of the 5th Dynasty pyramid of Unas at Saqqara,[12] and they documented and gave advice to the king on his journey into the afterlife. These inscriptions were later copied onto other pyramids from the Old Kingdom and have therefore survived in good

---

[12] Shaw 2015

condition.

Unas Pyramid Text

Possibly the next most influential source came from the Roman era. Plutarch was a Greek historian and priest who lived in the late 1st and early 2nd century CE. He traveled to Egypt, it seems, but once he arrived there he was incapable of reading any hieroglyphs, so he largely depended on conversations with the locals and also a smattering of earlier literature that speculated on the identity of Egyptian gods and compared them with the Greeks" own pantheon. For instance, to the ancient Greeks the god Amun was Zeus, and the same applied to Hermes and Thoth, Apollo and Horus, and Dionysus and Osiris. The connection between Greece and Egypt was an ancient one and continues to have an influence on modern readers since many of the cult centers of ancient Egypt are referred to by their ancient Greek names, such as Hermopolis the City of Hermes, rather than their ancient Egyptian names, most likely because of the troublesome nature of transliterating Egyptian words. Nevertheless, Plutarch's *On Isis and Osiris* is the fullest account of the key myth in Egyptian mythology and is the best-known version for modern scholarship too.[13]

Despite the fact that Plutarch's account is late in terms of the wider history of Egyptian mythology, it is a surprisingly accurate take on the formation of the myth of Isis and Osiris,

---

[13] Pinch 2001

dating back to around 600 years before his arrival.[14] Of course, this does not make it an accurate account of the much earlier story of Osiris, but since describing his death and dismemberment was not a taboo for a Greek, his later account did not suffer from the obliqueness of the early sources.

Moreover, although Plutarch was not an Egyptian, he was an excellent scholar of foreign mythology. For him, the reason for writing down the myth of Isis and Osiris was to try and find a "fundamental truth" to the myths of both his own culture (of which he was a priest at Delphi for the remaining 30 years of his life) and that of his neighboring culture, which all Greeks considered to be much more ancient than their own. It was his scholarly approach and earnest desire to record the 'truth" that makes his already interesting story worthy of study as a genuine account of the myth of Isis and Osiris.

---

[14] ibid.

A bust of Plutarch

The Gods as Concepts

Like in many polytheistic religious beliefs, the gods of ancient Egypt were neither omnipotent nor omnipresent, despite appearing in many locations simultaneously in some of the myths.[15] In fact, the ancient Egyptians used to worship the deity of the location they found themselves in, since each deity was more or less "present" in each part of the country. They were decidedly human in their relationships with each other. Just like the ancient Greek gods, they fought and argued, made love and married, and were ultimately capable of death, even if this meant that they would simply be reborn later on. Each god and goddess was "responsible" for an aspect of reality the ancient Egyptians encountered every day but, when they needed to, they could share their powers with another deity, which resulted in a kind of *merging* of the two. This was the case for the "dying sun god" who merged with Osiris so as to borrow his regenerative power and be "reborn" the following day.[16]

In the Memphite theology, the universe is created by the god Ptah, who "conceived the elements of creation in his heart and pronounced them into existence with the divine words as he pronounced their names." Yet some scholars believe that Ptah was only capable of such creation after he borrowed the heart and tongue from Amun, the ultimate creator; as such it was Ptah's being the personification of "creative process" that directed and guided Amun's creative abilities.[17]

When the deities merged or even appeared to take on the attributes of another god or goddess they were said to "literally become" the other deity. Shaw gives the example of Hathor attacking mankind with such a rage that she actually transformed into the bloodthirsty goddess Sekhmet. It might be best to think of the deities of ancient Egypt as manifestations rather than distinct personalities with concrete biographies. As such they helped the ancient Egyptians describe the world around them and, by giving precedents in their myths, explain away the more confusing aspects of why the world is the way it is.[18]

In ancient Egyptian culture the duality of deities – most often manifested in their male/female relationships – was an integral aspect of the belief system. This duality appeared in Nun, the limitless ocean of potentiality out of which the universe was born. Within those waters, the male and female aspects appeared as frogs (males) and snakes (females). There were four couples, according to the beliefs at Hermopolis, making up the eight most important gods of "pre-creation" referred to at this cult center as the "Ogdoad". Each of these gods and goddesses acquired names and, as a unit, they represented the earliest aspects of reality. Nun and Naunet

---

[15] Shaw 2015
[16] Shaw 2015
[17] Shaw 2015
[18] Shaw 2015

represented the "limitless waters" out of which everything was created; Huh and Hauhet represented the concept of "infinity"; Kuk and Kauket represented "darkness," and Amun and Amunet represented the concept of "hiddenness".[19] Later assessments of the Ogdoad, certainly by the time of the Theban attempt at "unification," emphasize the role of Amun in the creation of the first island and subsequently of the egg from which the sun god is hatched.

Atum's children, Shu and Tefnut, were also both siblings and a couple at the same time but their separation from their father led to the separation between an "above" and "below" by Shu, which created all of the space in which life could appear and grow. Also, Shu represented *neheh*, which was the Egyptian concept of cyclical time, whereas his wife came to represent *djet*, which was the concept of 'time at a standstill, covering everything that is remaining and lasting, such as mummies or stone architecture," according to Gary Shaw.[20]

In the coupling of the gods, Osiris and Isis were one of the earliest to have established their incestuous relationship with an apparent "wooing in the womb." Isis's role as a wife and mother is unlike any other in Egyptian mythology. The story of Osiris's death and resurrection is best read with Isis's agency in mind too. She is not an idle mourner of her husband, nor is she the mere receptacle of a divine birth. She actively seeks out Osiris's body, performing a magical ritual to acquire from the body enough of Osiris's 'seed" to conceive, and she even goes so far as to poison Re in order to learn his secret names and pass on their power to her child. Similar to Osiris, Isis is an instigator as much as a carer. If Osiris ensures the regeneration and rebirth of the sun, the dead and the crops beside the Nile, then none of those accomplishments would have been brought to fruition without Isis's unwavering perseverance to resurrect her husband. She is no ordinary "Queen" in the medieval European sense, she was proactive and, as such, defined Osiris as much as he defined her.

Now that the basics of Egyptian beliefs have been presented, the myths will hopefully become a little clearer, or at very least more contextualised. The ability to use original texts is a luxury that is available to modern readers thanks to the passionate and untiring work of translators and scholars around the world, an enormous job that still has vast veins of knowledge to uncover, and should not be forgotten when enjoying even the most cursory study of this beautiful mythology.

---

[19] Shaw 2015
[20] Shaw 2015

A statue of Osiris wearing an Atef-crown made of bronze

Statuettes of Osiris (middle) alongside Horus (left) and Isis (right)

The Mythological Landscape

The ibis-headed scribe of the ancient world remains one of the most enigmatic and influential deities ever to have been worshipped by people. Not being one of the terrifying deities like the fierce heart-eating, crocodile-headed Ammut, nor a king like Horus or Osiris, whose association with the sun deity gave them unusual importance in Egyptian belief at home and abroad, Thoth has occupied a strange place in the imagination of later readers of Egyptian history.

Nevertheless, Thoth influenced scholars and theologians since his earliest worship during the Pre-Dynastic Period, all the way through to the Renaissance and beyond.

The main reason for Thoth's lasting influence – as well as his prominence even during the earliest days of his worship – is that he embodies the human capacity for pursuing and even glorifying knowledge. Although Thoth did have mystical aspects, his knowledge (and therefore his magic) was of a predominantly functional sort. He was the god who invented those "holy symbols" or hieroglyphs, without which histories could not be written and the dead would become lost on their journey through the land of the dead. He was the god of magic, whose power could as easily protect and restore to life as it could decimate the land. And yet he was also the architect and enforcer of that universal law, just like the law of physics or mathematics that was immutable and unbiased. As such, Thoth represents the knowledgeable, authoritative force of nature. Potent, at times mysterious, but always adherent to a natural order.

To the ancient Egyptians the sun was the dominant figure in their mythology, but it is important to remember that it was also twinned with its less luminous brother, the moon. This duality was fixed and vital to the understanding of Thoth as a major deity in the Egyptian pantheon. He was not diminished by his association with the less brilliant orb that crossed the Egyptian sky, because to the Egyptians, the moon was a celestial clock that guided the rituals of the temples and recorded the passage of time by way of its uniformly changing aspects. In many respects, it is the perfect symbol of the dynamic god who began his "career" as a wrathful god capable of laying waste to those opponents of the universal law, or *maat*, and later became the impassive hero of truth and wisdom.

Given the fact that the worship of Thoth has been traced as far back as 6000 BCE, his biography has a tapestry of often conflicting "truths," further adding to his enigmatic personality. Depending on the cycle of myths the reader refers to, Thoth's parentage can be one such problematic truth. According to one version, he was the "son of two fathers," meaning that he was born to both Horus and Seth though this creates a chronological anomaly for many of the myths that have survived which place Thoth either protecting his "father" as a child or being present at the establishment of the cosmos.[21] Similarly, Thoth was often called the "god with no mother" and he was either depicted as simply emerging from the primordial waters or being born from the "lips of Re" to uphold *maat*. It was Thoth who created the "cosmic egg."[22]

It is known that Thoth, like many of the other gods in the pantheon, also had a female "counterpart" in the character of Seshat. Seshat's name literally means "she who inscribes/writes," and she was associated with many of the same tasks for which Thoth would later become most famous, including recording annals, writing spells, and enabling architects to design their temples and tombs with the same precision Thoth exacted of the universe. Where her

---

[21] Tyldesley 2011
[22] Pinch 2002

duties ceased and those of Thoth began is never clearly defined, but they are both aspects of the same supernatural and inspirational force. The ambiguity concerning Thoth's provenance and his "working" relationship with his female counterpart ultimately had little effect on his worship, as the great city of Hermopolis demonstrates.

Hermopolis Magna

Roland Unger's picture of the basilica, el-Ashmunein, in Hermopolis

Hermopolis Magna, or "the Great City of Hermes," is clearly a Greek name and, therefore, a later addition to the Thoth story, but this "foreign" name perfectly demonstrates the prominence of Thoth in this city. The ancient Egyptians' name for the city, Khmun, referred to the Ogdoad, or the eight principal deities of the cycle of myths associated with Hermopolis. The Ogdoad, similar to the Ennead, was made up of primordial gods who represented the esoteric aspects of that "time" such as darkness and lack of boundaries. There were often four gods twinned with their female counterparts to make the eight deities of the Ogdoad, with Thoth as its leader.[23]

By the time the ancient Greeks experienced this fantastic religious center, they saw that it was dominated by the figure they referred to as Hermes. This was a common practice amongst ancient polytheistic cultures, but encountering a "foreign" god caused less threat to the polytheistic cultures of the past than the monotheistic cultures of the present. To the ancients –

---

[23] Pinch 2002

and this was a practice employed by the Greeks, Romans and even as late as the Norse – a foreign god was merely another aspect of a deity they were already familiar with from their own pantheon. In the case of Thoth, the Greeks encountered a god of magic, writing (namely, hermeneutics), and knowledge who sometimes acted as a "messenger" of sorts for other deities, all aspects of their own god Hermes. Therefore, the Greeks believed Thoth was just another, older aspect of him.

Needless to say, the ancient Greeks were lenient in their interpretations despite the fact that certain aspects of "the Egyptian Hermes" must have been shocking in the least. For them, the young trickster god who stole cattle from Apollo was associated with many of the theoretical aspects of Thoth, and even one of the aesthetic aspects too: the snake. It has been suggested that Hermes was actually a "pre-Olympian" god, meaning his worship predates the establishment of the Greek pantheon as it is known today, and that he was originally a "snake-god."[24] If this is the case, then the Egyptian beliefs that Re left snakes on and under the Earth as testament to his magical power on Earth, and that Thoth would later come to be the ruler of such magic, mean the aesthetic connections between the two gods makes perfect sense. What would have been surprising to the Greeks, however, was Thoth's affiliation with the baboon.

At Thoth's principal temple in Hermopolis Magna, the entrance was flanked by a pair of colossal statues of baboons, an impressive sight to anybody who visited the temple. In symbolic terms, baboons are generally considered to be aggressive and lascivious, and this was certainly the case for the Egyptian baboon-headed god Babi who was associated with the potential virility and aggression of the dominant baboon in nature.[25]

A handful of theories have emerged to explain the connection between such a creature and Thoth. One such theory is that since baboons tended to let out a cacophony of shrieking early in the morning, they came to be associated with the figurative "dying" of the moon and the "rebirth" of the sun. If this was the case, then certainly they would have had a vague, temporal connection with Thoth.

However, it seems more likely that it was the physical attributes of the baboon that had an influence. Thoth appears in the form of the baboon sitting atop the scales on which the heart of the dead was weighed against the feather of *maat*. Thoth's role in the rituals of death was that of a scribe, first and foremost, and the theory suggests that the dexterity of baboons' hands lent itself easily to a connection between the baboon and the most dexterous scribe in existence.[26] Whatever the truth may be, the importance of writing and scripture at Hermopolis is evident in the material record of that great site.

---

[24] Frothingham 1916
[25] Pinch 2002
[26] ibid.

Steven G. Johnson's picture of a statue of Thoth depicted as a baboon dating back to
1500 BCE

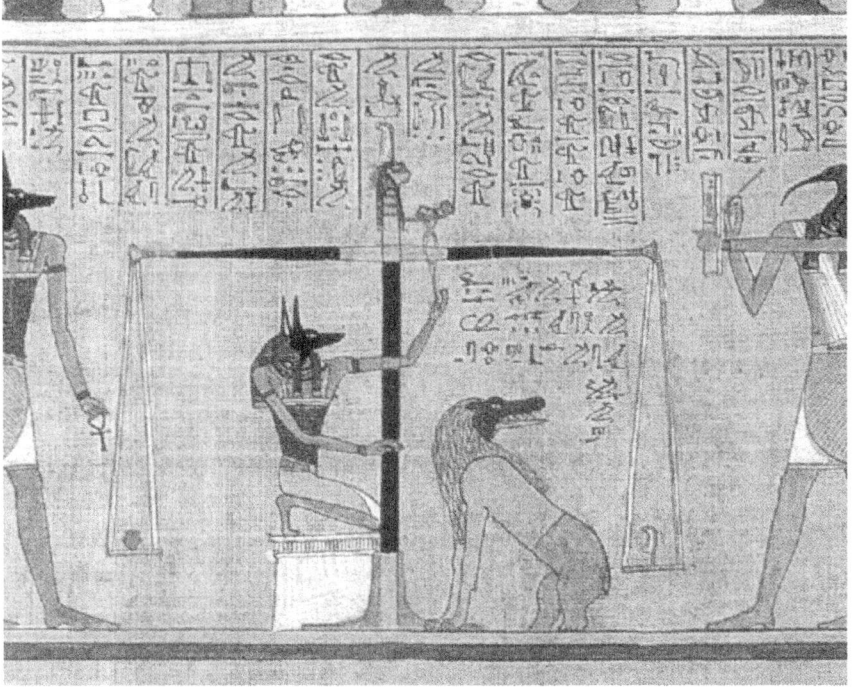

A tomb depiction of the heart being weighed

The lauded Church scholar Clement of Alexandria, writing in the 2nd century CE, produce a number of works on how Christians should think, act and approach their own history. One such work was called the *Stromata*, in which Clement attempts to defend the primacy of Judeo-Christian thought over the accomplishments of the Greek philosophers. By way of showing their adoption of Egyptian ideas, Clement tried to prove that the Greeks had a penchant for plagiarism and "appropriated their most excellent dogmas" from the Judeo-Christian tradition. This largely incorrect diatribe nevertheless resulted in Clement recording the existence of the quasi-mystical Book of Thoth and its supposed contents.

Referring to Thoth in the style of the Greeks, Clement noted the uniqueness of Egyptian religion and philosophy: "For the Egyptians pursue a philosophy of their own. This is principally shown by their sacred ceremonial. For first advances the Singer, bearing some one of the symbols of music. For they say that he must learn two of the books of Hermes, the one of which contains the hymns of the gods, the second the regulations for the king's life. And after the Singer advances the Astrologer, with a horologe in his hand, and a palm, the symbols of astrology. He must have the astrological books of Hermes, which are four in number, always in his mouth. Of these, one is about the order of the fixed stars that are visible, and another about the conjunctions and luminous appearances of the sun and moon; and the rest respecting their risings. Next in order advances the sacred Scribe, with wings on his head, and in his hand a book and rule, in which were writing ink and the reed, with which they write. And he must be acquainted with what are called hieroglyphics, and know about cosmography and geography, the position of the sun and moon, and about the five planets; also the description of Egypt, and the chart of the Nile; and the description of the equipment of the priests and of the places consecrated to them, and about the measures and the things in use in the sacred rites. Then the Stole-keeper follows those previously mentioned, with the cubit of justice and the cup for libations. He is acquainted with all points called Pædeutic (relating to training) and Moschophatic (sacrificial). There are also ten books which relate to the honour paid by them to their gods, and containing the Egyptian worship; as that relating to sacrifices, first-fruits, hymns, prayers, processions, festivals, and the like. And behind all walks the Prophet, with the water-vase carried openly in his arms; who is followed by those who carry the issue of loaves. He, as being the governor of the temple, learns the ten books called "Hieratic;" and they contain all about the laws, and the gods, and the whole of the training of the priests. For the Prophet is, among the Egyptians, also over the distribution of the revenues. There are then forty-two books of Hermes indispensably necessary; of which the six-and-thirty containing the whole philosophy of the Egyptians are learned by the forementioned personages; and the other six, which are medical, by the Pastophoroi (image-bearers),—treating of the structure of the body, and of diseases, and instruments, and medicines, and about the eyes, and the last about women. Such are the customs of the Egyptians, to speak briefly."[27]

In these 42 books of Thoth/Hermes, Clement found – whether he wished to or not – the fundamental aspects of the Egyptian god of knowledge and wisdom. Curiously enough, despite the fact that a single "Book of Thoth" has arguably never been found, the vast majority of the Coffin Texts were found in Middle Egypt, in and around the city of Hermopolis, and Thoth and the rest of the Ogdoad featured heavily in these texts.[28] It is clear, then, that Thoth's principal seat of worship was also a producer of fine texts from as early as the 2nd millennium BCE, suggesting a strong connection between his worship and the skill he was supposed to have inspired.

[27] Roberts & Donaldson 1885
[28] Pinch 2002

The Solar Barque and Apophis

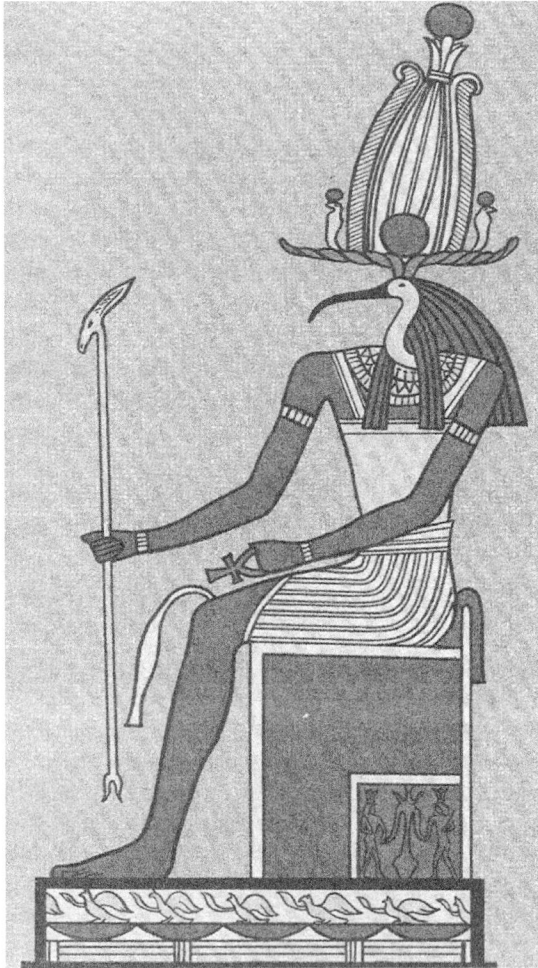

A depiction of Thoth on a throne

The story of the "Solar Barque" or the boat of Re, is one of the principal features of Egyptian mythology since it not only embodies the prominence Re held in the religious mindset but it also serves as a good example of the ancient Egyptian concept of cyclical time.

Ancient Egyptians believed that Re traversed the sky each day in a glorious barque equipped with a highly trained crew of deities that guaranteed its safe passage. Once the zenith had been reached, the barque would slip down the sky towards the West, where lay the dreaded entrance to the land of the dead, the Duat. At the horizon, Re and his crew would change into the "night boat" called the Mesketet. Although it still belonged to Re, and therefore was still the 'sun boat," the Mesketet was named as such because it was associated with "perishing" as Re was said to enter the land of the dead and die there (temporarily).[29] To the ancient Egyptians, the Duat was no blissful land of rest. It was a sprawling terrain that spanned the underworld from the West to the East and it was replete with dangers that threatened the re-emergence (and effective "re-birth") of Re and the sun that was the source of all life in the land of the living.

This kind of story is indicative of acclaimed mythologist G. S. Kirk's second definition of myth as an "operative, iterative or validatory" story, the type of which "[tended] to be repeated regularly on ritual or ceremonial occasions … to bring about a desirable continuity in nature or society."[30] It was the role of the priests to repeat this story each day, most probably with supporting rituals to aid its efficacy, so as to ensure the continuation of the cosmos. Naturally, this is not unique to Egyptian mythology but the role of Seth in its proceedings is particularly interesting.

The god of disorder and chaos boarded the Solar Barque each day and took a place of prominence on it at the bow. Alongside a cadre of other deities, including the sister he tormented and the nephew who would be his greatest adversary among the gods, Seth took up his scepter and an iron lance and embarked on the perilous journey. The surviving sources tell of a journey of 12 hours that involved the cadre of deities having to vanquish the enemies of Re and his boat with the help of a variety of divine aids, from fire-spitting cobras to the ancient god Aker "whose two sphinx-like heads face away from each other at either end of his flat body."[31] It is at the 7th hour, however, that the barque encounters its most formidable enemy, the great serpent Apophis.

Seth's connection with Apophis is an integral one to Egyptian mythology and shows Seth to be more virtuous than he was later depicted. Seth was the strongest of the gods, and, as such, he had a prestigious place on the great "Solar Barque" that traversed the skies each day and contended with the perilous land of the dead, the Duat, at night. To the ancient Egyptians the rising of the sun was not a guaranteed phenomenon each day, and many of the spells and rituals recorded in the surviving literature attests to the fragility of the cosmos and the priests' role in maintaining it.[32] The Duat, although ruled by the benevolent Osiris, was seen as a land of dangerous monsters and demons and so the Solar Barque needed Seth at its prow to protect it.

The ancient Egyptians told the story of the progression of the Solar Barque through Duat by

[29] Tyldesley 2011
[30] Kirk 1996
[31] Tyldesley 2011
[32] Pinch 2002

the hours of the night. Each hour was like an episode in the divine adventure and each episode had its gatekeeper and its challenges. At the 7th and 12th hours, however, the Solar Barque encountered its most feared monster of all: Apophis. Depending on the source, Apophis is either depicted as a great crocodile or, most commonly, as an enormous serpent. He was said to have been born from Neith's saliva while she was still in the eternal waters of Nun and, being a monster of discord, he began his life by trying unsuccessfully to swallow the eternal waters and stop the universe from coming into being at the onset.

Apophis is, essentially, the manifestation of chaos. He embodied the Egyptian concept of isfet in every action and appearance in the mythology. By trying to impede the Solar Barque on its natural journey, Apophis' role was that of interrupting the natural state of the universe, maat. The duality here is unmistakable but the earlier myths allow for a level of cognitive dissonance too. For instance, to the ancient Egyptians the snake was a symbol of protection and of rebirth and renewal but, in the case of Apophis, the symbol was flipped on its head in order to provide the gods with their ultimate adversary. This dissonance was not unique in this myth, however, as the role of Seth, Horus' and Osiris' great adversary, was also inverted since he was the champion of Re and the 'slayer of the enemy of Pre daily." It would seem that the ancient Egyptians were quite comfortable with this level of dissonance, or at least irregularity, in their myths but as time went on the lines became less blurred and Seth's and Apophis' roles came into starker contrast with the world of maat.

An Egyptian depiction of Seth spearing the serpent Apophis

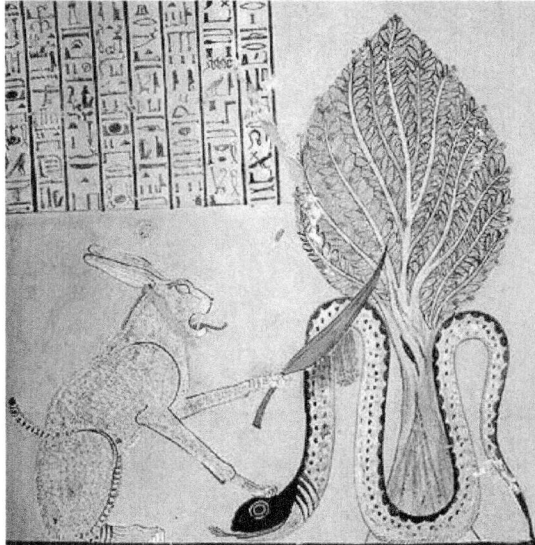

A depiction of Ra, in the form of a cat, spearing Apophis

Vocabulary concerning Apophis had obvious repercussions outside of Egypt. Named the "Rebel" or the "Great Adversary" or even the "Evil One," Apophis' influence on later Christian ideas of their own "Adversary" is unmistakable. However, the ancient Greeks were no less influenced by this great snake, although the characters of Apophis and Seth became more intertwined. In Greco-Roman period Seth came to be associated with the very chaos beast he was known to the Egyptians as defeating.[33] When Plutarch was writing, he often used the name of Typhon to describe Seth, but Typhon/Python was the most fearsome serpentine monster of Greek mythology, not he that defeated it. Therein lies the confusion behind the nomenclature, since it was the Greek god Apollo who was associated with fighting Typhon, as related in the Homeric Hymn to that god:

> "And thereafter [Hera] never came to the bed of wise Zeus for a full year ... But when the months and days were fulfilled and the seasons duly came on as the earth moved round, she bore one neither like the gods nor mortal men, fell, cruel Typhaon, to be a plague to men. Straightway large-eyed queenly Hera took him and bringing one evil thing to another such, gave him to the dragoness; and she received him. And this Typhon used to work great mischief among the famous tribes of men. Whosoever met the dragoness, the day of doom would sweep him away, until the

---

[33] ibid.

lord Apollo, who deals death from afar, shot a strong arrow at her. Then she, rent with bitter pangs, lay drawing great gasps for breath and rolling about that place. An awful noise swelled up unspeakable as she writhed continually this way and that amid the wood: and so she left her life, breathing it forth in blood. Then Phoebus Apollo boasted over her: 'Now rot here upon the soil that feeds man. You at least shall live no more to be a fell bane to men who eat the fruit of the all-nourishing earth, and who will bring hither perfect hecatombs. Against cruel death neither Typhoeus shall avail you nor ill-famed Chimera, but here shall the Earth and shining Hyperion make you rot.'

"Thus said Phoebus, exulting over her: and darkness covered her eyes. And the holy strength of Helios made her rot away there; wherefore the place is now called Pytho, and men call the lord Apollo by another name, Pythian; because on that spot the power of piercing Helios made the monster rot away."[34]

When the ancient Greeks came into contact with the ancient Egyptians and learned of their mythology, they instantly saw the figure of Apollo in Horus, whose victory over his father's killer Seth (equated to Typhon/Python) was celebrated every year by driving wild asses over a precipice.[35] In the case of the Homeric Hymn, Typhon is defeated by Helios, the Greek god of the sun, and the "all-nourishing earth" that was integral to the Egyptian notion of maat was rid of its "bane" forever more. This story is of distinctly Greek design, rather than Egyptian. The merging of Seth and Apophis to produce the character of Typhon, as well as the lack of a cyclical battle between good and evil, are just two examples of why this is so. And yet there is another, euhemeristic theory that some scholars have pointed out to make sense of the Egyptian version too.

Interestingly, the Hyksos kings mentioned above who invaded and occupied the Nile Delta around the 17th century BCE included among themselves one king who went by the name of Apophis. As legend has it, King Apophis provoked the king at Thebes to fight a war that would ultimately result in the Hyksos people being driven out of Egypt by those from Thebes. It's not much of a legend, but what can be seen in this story is the mythologizing of a real-world conflict. The Hyksos people being driven out by kings of Thebes does not inspire much poetic or religious thinking, but it does when the conflict is represented as a battle between the forces of two distinct gods. Since the "foreigners" of the Nile Delta worshipped Seth (or, in this case the Canaanite occupiers worshipped his equivalent, Baal) and the forces of Thebes were known for their worship of Horus, the real-world battle became a symbolic battle between the two gods from their land.[36]

---

[34] *Hymn to Apollo* 349ff
[35] Graves 1955
[36] Pinch 2002

Curiously, there are some scholars who see an influence from the ancient Egyptian depictions of Seth and Apophis in a much later Christian myth. Due to the occasional depiction of Apophis as a crocodile-serpent hybrid, it has been suggested that Apophis was one of the precursors of the western dragon and Seth, wielding his iron lance and defeating the beast under foot, has been connected with that ubiquitous saint George of dragon-slaying fame. This would not be the only – nor the most far-fetched – influence Egyptian art and thought had on later Christianity, but it certainly is an emotive one that continues to be felt and utilised today.

Egyptian religion was beautifully crafted to allow for the occurrence of tragedy. The permanent and irrefutable presence of *ismet* alongside *maat* in the cosmos ensured this, and the pantheons were so beautifully crafted that there was almost always a spell, song, rite or defending deity to ensure that the mechanics of the universe continued to function. For the Solar Barque, the obvious protective figure is Seth since he was the quintessential warrior against the serpent of chaos, Apophis. However, it was said that Thoth and the personified version of *maat* stood either side of the barque too and this is no unimportant feature of the solar barque myth.

Much of what the Egyptians believed and practiced revolved around the progress of time. While the solar barque traversed the land of the dead, the Duat, the deities on board encountered a gate for each of the 12 hours of the night, and each hour brought with it a new challenge and a new dramatic event. The regulation of time was important to ancient Egyptian beliefs, and Thoth was at the center of all timekeeping, from the length of a human's life to the monthly schedule of rituals in the temple. The ancient Egyptians believed that dusk was the most dangerous time of the day – at least theologically if nothing else – since that was the moment their gods began their dangerous journey, but having Thoth and Maat guide the solar barque would no doubt have reassured the worried worshipper since Thoth was the god that orchestrated and ordained the mechanics of the universe. This didn't guarantee the barque's safety, of course, but the cadre of powerful gods that made up the entourage made the presence of ismet less menacing at least.

There is an interesting story about Thoth's time on the solar barque. It recounts the moment when Isis, mother of the great god Horus, is protecting her son from his wicked uncle Seth's plans to murder the only other heir to the throne. While hiding in the marshes of Khemmis, Isis returned from scavenging for food only to find that her darling child had been bitten by some kind of poisonous animal and was now lying almost lifeless on the riverbank. Isis let off a lamenting cry that reached the solar barque and eventually caused it to stop mid-journey through the sky. It was Thoth who traveled down from the sky to see what the problem was. When he arrived, he was berated by Isis for making plans and taking no action, however this time he had done more than simply plan, he had come equipped with the "Breath of Life" to restore the young god. Thoth recited spells and performed sacred rituals that bound Horus's protection with many natural features and animals in the world,[37] and then he returned to the solar barque and the sun-disk continued on its journey.

---

[37] Shaw 2015

Thoth explained his treatment of Horus by claiming he understood the importance of this young god for Isis, himself, and the rest of the gods. Obviously, this is a small myth within the greater story of Osiris, and subsequently the establishment of the royal line of Egyptian kings. Horus would grow up and battle his uncle for the inheritance of the throne and, in doing so, would bind the royal line to an order of succession from father to son, not brother to brother. By saving Horus, Thoth, who established the universal law and fate, sanctified Horus's claim to the throne and also gave divine authority to the inevitable establishment of the real-world royal line of kings. Such was the power and influence of the scribe of the universe.

The Arbitrator of The Gods

The title of "Arbitrator of the Gods" is a difficult one to define for Thoth. It is true that, at times, he stood between two opposing gods in order to ensure the arrival at a compromise that would maintain the balance between isfet and maat. However, there are much more interesting stories that show his more developed character. Two myths in particular reveal Thoth's character while also giving a good sense of the dynamics and power struggles within the Egyptian pantheon.

The story of Isis, Horus and Seth is possibly one of the most famous of all ancient Egyptian myths. The reason for this is that – aside from being alluded to in many other texts, inscriptions, and art – it appears in one of the fullest and most elaborate myths available to modern scholars, "The Contendings of Horus and Seth." Written towards the end of the 2nd millennium BCE, the Contendings begins with a debate between two groups of deities over who is worthier of the throne, the inexperienced Horus or the brother of the former king, Seth. Re, who presided over the debate, actually took Seth's side in the proceedings, so it was necessary to resort to an even higher authority to find an arbitrator.

This was not Thoth, though. Just as he implied when he revived the baby Horus as a child, Thoth supported Horus's claim to the throne. However, although he supported Horus, he obeyed Re's commands to write letters to various other deities when Re's own favorite failed to gain the support of the rest of the gods and goddesses. It is unclear why Re does not just overrule the rest of the gods, but it's most likely that this episode echoes the famously arduous legislative process of ancient Egypt.[38]

Thoth's role as an "impartial" scribe really comes to the forefront in this myth. Only he is trusted to write letters to the deities that aren't present, and his stylus appears to have no geographical bounds since he even manages to send a letter to Osiris in the Duat. A series of tedious affirmations of Horus's right to the throne come from the deities Thoth wrote to, all of which are repudiated by Re, who ends up lying on the floor of his pavilion like a petulant child. Seth even manages to gouge out Horus's eyes at one point before both gods are ordered to make

---

[38] Tyldesley 2011

peace:

"Then they were brought before the Ennead. Said the Universal Lord before the Great Ennead to Horus and Seth: 'Go and obey what I tell you. You should eat and drink so that we may have (some) peace. Stop quarreling so every day on end.'

Then Seth told Horus: 'Come, let's make holiday in my house.'

Horus told him: 'I'll do so, surely, I'll do so, I'll do so.'

Now afterward, (at) evening time, bed was prepared for them, and they both lay down. But during the night, Seth caused his phallus to become stiff and inserted it between Horus's thighs. Then Horus placed his hands between his thighs and received Seth's semen. Horus went to tell his mother Isis: 'Help me, Isis, my mother, come and see what Seth has done to me.'

And he opened his hand(s) and let her see Seth's semen. She let out a loud shriek, seized the copper (knife), cut off his hand(s) that were equivalent. Then she fetched some fragrant ointment and applied it to Horus's phallus. She caused it to become stiff and inserted it into a pot, and he caused his semen to flow down into it.

Isis at morning time went carrying the semen of Horus to the garden of Seth and said to Seth's gardener: 'What sort of vegetable is it that Seth eats here in your company?'

So the gardener told her: 'He doesn't eat any vegetable here in my company except lettuce.'

And Isis added the semen of Horus onto it. Seth returned according to his daily habit and ate the lettuce, which he regularly ate. Thereupon he became pregnant with the semen of Horus. So Seth went to tell Horus: 'Come, let's go and I may contend with you in the tribunal.'

Horus told him: 'I'll do so, surely, I'll do so, I'll do so.'

They both went to the tribunal and stood in the presence of the Great Ennead. They were told: 'Speak concerning yourselves.'

Said Seth: 'Let me be awarded the office of Ruler, l.p.h., for as to Horus, the one who is standing (trial), I have performed the labor of a male against him.'

The Ennead let out a load cry. They spewed and spat at Horus's face. Horus laughed at them. Horus then took an oath by god as follows: 'All that Seth has said is false. Let Seth's semen be summoned that we may see from where it answers, and my own be summoned that we may see from where it answers.'

Then Thoth, lord of script and scribe of truth for the Ennead, put his hand on Horus's shoulder and said: 'Come out, you semen of Seth.'

And it answered him from the water in the interior of the marsh. Thoth put his hand on Seth's shoulder and said: 'Come out, you semen of Horus.'

Then it said to him: 'Where shall I come from?'

Thoth said to it: 'Come out from his ear.'

Thereupon it said to him: 'Is it from his ear that I should issue forth, seeing that I am divine seed?'

Then Thoth said to it:'Come out from the top of his head.'

And it emerged as a golden solar disk upon Seth's head. Seth became exceeding furious and extended his hand(s) to seize the golden solar disk. Thoth took it away from him and placed it as a crown upon his (own) head. Then the Ennead said: 'Horus is right, and Seth is wrong.'"[39]

That it is Thoth who finally reveals the truth behind Seth's lies is not arbitrary at all. Lies were a form of isfet and Thoth, rather than denounce Seth with no evidence, uses his magic to reveal the truth unequivocally. Moreover, by placing the "halo" around Horus' head, Thoth is not only revealing the truth but also "crowning" the new king and establishing him as the "true heir to the creator sun god."[40] Once again, Thoth defines the laws of the universe (in this case, the laws of Egypt, which were one and the same to the ancient residents of that land) not through his own authority but through his ability to witness maat and document its presence.

The "Eye of Re" is another aspect of ancient Egyptian mythology that is often confusingly multi-faceted. At times it belongs to Re, but at others it doesn't at all. Sometimes, as is the case in the episode of "the Distant Goddess," it takes on human form and characteristics and is completely at odds with its "owner" Re. The common theme running throughout the stories of the Eye of Re, however, is that of its power and ferocity, and this is the basis of the myth of the Distant Goddess.

As the story goes, Re's eye became furious with him either because he replaced her with another eye or because he betrayed her after she punished humanity for him. Nevertheless, she fled to the Nubian Desert, where she could unleash her fury in the wilderness and become "the Distant Goddess." None of the deities, not even the all-powerful Re, was prepared to take on the unbridled fury of the Distant Goddess. The reason for this was that Re was only "all-powerful" because he possessed the one weapon that could defeat any enemy and was the source of Re's protection: the Eye. Without the Eye, Re was vulnerable, but, more importantly, without her master to direct and guide her, the universe was vulnerable to the wrath of the Eye. This is why none of the deities wished to search for the Distant Goddess and risk incurring her wrath, except for Thoth.

Now, Thoth did not prepare for his journey like some knight errant in a troubadour's song. In fact, he did not seem to prepare for battle at all. Instead, he sought out the Distant Goddess armed with only his mind and magic. Thoth took the form of the baboon and scoured the desert looking for the formidable Goddess. When he found her in the Nubian Desert, he initially tried to

---

[39] Simpson trans. 1972
[40] Pinch 2002

convince her to return by ensuring her that she was not only respected among the other gods but that her role as the Eye of Re was integral to the natural order of things. It is said that Thoth asked the Goddess no fewer than 1,077 times to come home, demonstrating his talent for persistence and unwillingness to give up.[41] Nevertheless, this line of reasoning did not persuade the Distant Goddess, and she reacted by showing Thoth one of her most terrifying aspects: a fire-breathing lioness. This scared Thoth, who was fearful yet respectful of the goddess.

With that, Thoth decided to change his tack and persuade her another way. What followed was a series of fables implying that her destructive anger balanced the justice of *maat*, and that without it, the universe would fall into chaos.[42] One of his fables went on to influence that great inventor of fables, Aesop. According to Aesop's fable, there was once a lion that was so ferocious and terrifying that all of the creatures around him feared and respected him. He used to roam the wilderness looking for prey, but one day he came across a bedraggled panther limping along his path. The panther's skin was torn and his fur was left in tatters, so the lion asked the poor creature who had done this to him. The panther replied that man had done it, and continued on its way.

The lion continued walking, and as he did he came across cows, oxen, donkeys, and horses all chained up and mistreated like the panther had been. The lion surveyed the pitiful creatures in shock, but when he came across a mighty bear and a lion in the same condition, he vowed to make man suffer for what he had done to his brethren. It was during this declaration of vengeance that a small mouse ran under the lion's foot. The mouse begged the lion to spare its life, so that it may one day repay the lion with some service he could offer. The lion, seeing that the mouse would hardly satisfy his appetite, laughed at the mouse's presumption and let it go.

The lion left the poor creatures and went in search of the culprit. He had planned on unleashing the fullness of his strength and ferocity on "man," but he underestimated man's cunning and soon found himself falling into a trap with a binding net of crossed leather falling on top of him. The lion roared and fought with the net, but it was the mouse who came to his aid and was able to gnaw through the leather straps and set him free. When the lion asked why the mouse helped him, the mouse said, "It is beautiful to do good."[43]

The story in its own right has enough aesthetic quality to ensure its survival through the centuries, later to be written down and amended slightly by Aesop, but the Egyptian version has some notable religious aspects worthy of mentioning. First, Thoth's persistence is paramount to the religious tale of him and the Distant Goddess. Showing that he asked the ferocious goddess 1,077 times makes Thoth a hero in a very mythological way. It was a common theme for goddesses in later myths (such as the Greek and Roman variants), but in Egyptian mythology,

---

[41] ibid.
[42] ibid.
[43] ibid.

persistence and resilience were common heroic attributes. This is even more important since, in Egyptian mythology, the hero was often a magician. It is possible that this narrative trait was established by the story of Thoth's adventure with the Distant Goddess, but even if it wasn't, the story certainly gives those attributes a powerful pedigree.

Another aspect worthy of mention is Thoth's taking the form of a baboon in order to search for the Distant Goddess. There is an association between Thoth, the fire-breathing goddess, and the underworld since there was said to be four baboons "with scorching breath" that guarded the Lake of Fire in the underworld.[44] These baboons were also judges of the dead, so what can be seen in this tale is Thoth traversing an unwelcoming desert in order to face a supernatural power that may spell his destruction if he is not wise. In this way, the story of the Distant Goddess sets a precedent for Thoth's role in the preparation of the dead for their perilous journey through the Duat.

In the end, Thoth does manage to convince the Distant Goddess to return "home," and, in doing so, he restores the second powerful eye in his "career." The restoration of both Re's and Horus's eyes are pivotal episodes in Egyptian mythology, and that Thoth is the restorer of these fundamental aspects of power places him in the focal role of the universe. Thoth does not take sides - he provides balance, which is what the universe requires to function.

Judge of the Dead

"To which god shall I announce you?"

"To him who is now present. Tell it to the Dragoman of the Two Lands."

"Who is the Dragoman of the Two Lands?"

"He is Thoth."[45]

In the popular imagination, there is little recollection of the importance of Thoth's role in the judging of the dead. This is perhaps understandable since the principal deity the dead has to address is Osiris, and the defining moment is the weighing of the heart against *maat*. However, it should have become obvious by now that Thoth and *maat* were inseparable in the minds of the ancient Egyptians, so Thoth not only inscribed the results of the dead's appeal to *maat* but, in doing so, participated in the judgment too.

The dead were believed to travel across the dangerous Duat after they passed on, and much of surviving religious texts were dedicated to aiding them on this journey. These texts take many forms, but the most famous "text" is known today as "The Book of the Dead." Originally the

---

[44] ibid.
[45] Spell 125 Book of the Dead, all texts from Faulkner translation 2001

book was called "The Book of Coming Forth by Day," but that name has fallen out of use.

The text was originally believed to have been one of the many written by Thoth himself. It consists of almost 200 spells of varying length that were given to the dead in order to prepare them for their journey, and also to purge their earthly souls of the mortal detritus that made them unclean. In the spells, Thoth is granted almost unlimited power in the Underworld, similar to both Osiris and Re who are appealed to regularly. One of the reasons for Thoth's equivalence with the great gods of the pantheon is that he was given the charge of decreeing the length of all creatures' lives.[46]

A tomb depiction of the weighing of the heart

According to Spell 175, Thoth was granted this task after the gods saw the misdeeds of men: "O Thoth, what is it that has come about through the Children of Nut [Here, Humans] They have made war, they have raised up tumult, they have done slaughter, they have created imprisonment, they have reduced what was great to what is little in all that we have made; show greatness, O Thoth - so says Atum. You shall not witness wrongdoing, you shall not suffer it! Shorten their years, cut short their months, because they have done hidden damage to all that you have made. I have your palette, O Thoth, I bring your inkpot to you …"[47]

---

[46] Pinch 2002
[47] trans. Faulkner 2001

Thoth's "inkpot" here is the inkpot of the universe. The vessel from which he wrote the immutable laws of the universe and therefore one such immutable law was the lifespan of a human. In this case, Thoth's "inscriptions" are not just records but decrees, and his role is most certainly an active one.

Thoth was often depicted in his ibis-headed form during the judgment of a dead person's heart, but he also often appeared in the form of A'an, the baboon. This creature would sit atop the scales, and it was he who declared whether the heart was just enough to tip the scales in its favour against the feather of *maat*.

A depiction of Thoth's declaration to the Ennead, based on the weighing of the heart of the scribe Ani

Spell 125 describes what appears to be the moment before the deceased's heart is measured against the feather of maat. The great translator R.O. Faulkner said of the spell, "The deceased declares to the tribunal of forty-two gods that he has not committed a series of specified sins which in Egyptian eyes apparently covered every conceivable kind of wrong-doing. The declaration, long known by the self-contradictory title of 'The Negative Confession,' is better named 'The Declaration of Innocence.'"[48] The spell is, essentially, a formula for "descending to the great hall of the Double Maat," in which the deceased found themselves before the throne of Osiris, surrounded by a jury of other gods and goddesses, to whom they had to defend themselves of a litany of sins. Since most of these sins were of a religious nature, it's likely that the entire episode is a remnant of an initiation ritual for the priesthood.[49]

The spell begins with a throat-clearing on the part of the deceased, in which they give a general

---

[48] 2001
[49] Pinch 2002

round-up of the sins they have not committed: "Behold I have come to you, I have brought you truth, I have repelled falsehood for you. I have not done falsehood against men, I have not impoverished my associates, I have done no wrong in the Place of Truth, I have not learnt that which is not, I have done no evil, I have not daily made labour in excess of what was due to be done for me, my name has not reached the offices of those who control salves, I have not deprived the orphan of his property …"

After this comes specific "declarations of innocence" to each of the 42 gods in the "tribunal," each of which includes a kind of epithet and the place where the god "originated," probably meaning their main seat of worship.

In the case of Thoth, he is referred to in the following way: "O Nosey who came from Hermopolis, I have not been rapacious." This is a fairly comical way of referring to the god, but it is most likely just a reference to the ibis beak that was associated with him.

A selection of declarations follows here to give a sense of the format of the spell:

"Oh Swallower of shades who came forth from the cavern, I have not stolen. "

"Oh Dangerous One who came forth from Rosetjau, I have not killed men. "

"Oh Double Lion who came forth from the sky, I have no destroyed food-supplies. "

"Oh Fiery Eyes who came forth from Letopolis, I have done no crookedness. "

"Oh Flame which came forth backwards, I have not stolen the god's offerings. "

"Oh Bone-breaker who came forth from Heracleopolis, I have not told lies. "

"Oh Green of flame who came forth from Memphis, I have not taken food. "

"Oh You of the cavern who came forth from the West, I have not been sullen. "

"Oh White of teeth who came forth from Faiyum, I have not transgressed. "

"Oh Blood-eater who came forth from the shambles, I have not killed a sacred bull. "

"Oh Eater of entrails who came forth from the House of Thirty, I have not committed perjury."[50]

The deceased is then questioned by the gods, and he or she must respond in accordance with the innocence they have just declared. In particular, the deceased addresses the "Dragoman of the Two Lands." Thoth then replies to the deceased:

---

[50] Faulkner 2001

"Come," says Thoth. "What have you come for?"

"I have come here to report."

"What is your condition?"

"I am pure from evil, I have excluded myself from the quarrels of those who are now living, I am not among them."

Thoth then announces the deceased to Osiris, to whom he or she will go to have their heart judged against the feather of maat.

Spell 30B is often titled "The Judgement of the Dead" since it describes the weighing of the heart against the feather of *maat*, often called the "Feather of Righteousness" in this context. It opens with one of the most famous exhortations on the part of the deceased: "Oh my heart which I had from my mother! O my heart of my different ages! Do not stand up as a witness against me, do not be opposed to me in the tribunal do not be hostile to me in the presence of the Keeper of the Balance, for you are my ka which was in my body, the protector who made my members hale. Go forth to the happy place whereto we speed; do not make my name stink to the Entourage who make men. Do not tell lies about me in the presence of the god …"[51]

There is a strange cynicism here that could either be the fruit of a guilty conscience, or simply an acceptance of the inevitable presence of "ill-deeds" (to a certain degree) in life. Thus, the spell may have been written to remind the deceased person's heart to think only of the "righteous" acts. In the case of the dead's heart not being judged as sinless, the person would then appeal to Thoth to argue on their behalf.[52]

According to the text, the following happens in the case of the heart being "righteous." "Thus says Thoth, judge of truth, to the Great Ennead which is in the presence of Osiris: Hear this word of very truth. I have judged the heart of the deceased, and his soul stands as a witness for him. His deeds are righteous in the great balance, and no sin has been found in him…"[53] Notice that Thoth says here that he has judged the heart, but that the deeds were "righteous in the great balance," meaning Thoth's judgment was not a personal one but an "empirical" one according to universal law. Geraldine Pinch described the journey of the soul in language that represented this assimilation with a "universal law": "the goal of the journey was to be transformed into an akh, an "effective" or "transfigured" spirit. Those who failed to justify their existence in the divine court faced a second death in the jaws of the Eater of Souls. The fortunate spirits could take their place among the stars or among the followers of Osiris, Ra, Thoth, or Hathor …"[54]

---

[51] Faulkner 2001
[52] Pinch 2002
[53] Faulkner 2001
[54] Pinch 2002

To the ancient Egyptians, *maat* was the ultimate judge of a dead person's heart, but it was also the source of regenerative powers given to the gods and those humans who were capable of traversing the Underworld and winning eternal life. Furthermore, it took on an ambrosial quality since the gods were said to "live on *maat*," as if it were their food and drink and the very air they breathed. It was the ancient Egyptian name for the unalterable laws of the universe, laws transcribed by Thoth himself.

Thoth's role in the afterlife was exceedingly important not just on the celestial level but on the human plane too. The dead person was said to fly to the heavens on Thoth's wings. His mansion was a safe place for the soul to rest and learn the magic that would aid them in their journey from there. This knowledge – as with many of the funerary spells – was generally considered to be the work of Thoth. As a god of knowledge, Thoth epitomized the curiosity and ingenuity of this highly advanced civilization, and, as such, he was present in all aspects of Egyptian life.

The Scientist

It was Thoth's calculations that set in motion the universe, its orbs, and laws, and his female counterpart Maat ensured its continued function. After this primacy, it seems that Thoth dedicated himself to revealing and producing knowledge for humankind. He gave his name to all advances in knowledge, from science to magic and all aspects of philosophy and theology in between. Since he set the universe in motion he was also the natural patron of astronomy and astrology too but the Egyptians took the movement of the heavens increasingly seriously and therefore Thoth became the god of mathematics and geometry too. One of the most commonly held assertions across Egypt was that Osiris, one of the first and greatest divine kings of Egypt credited with the invention of such wonders as the production and enjoyment of wine, consulted Thoth on every matter and even ensured that Thoth would be there for Isis as counsel when Osiris went traveling.[55]

Timekeeping was of particular importance to the ancient Egyptians. This was not simply because predicting the weather conditions lead to the richness of Egypt's fertile "Black Land" (agriculture was also a realm of Thoth's knowledge), but also because it dictated the complex temple festivals and rituals. The clearest connection between Thoth and the establishment of time is the story of his game of draughts with the moon, during which he "won from her the seventieth part of each of her periods of illumination, and from all the winnings he composed five days, and intercalated them as an addition to the three hundred and sixty days."[56] That the Egyptians later celebrated those days as the birthdays of the gods gives an idea of the sancrosanct nature of time, and it also shows that the ancient Egyptians had a clear concept of timekeeping that was invariably associated with the moon.

---

[55] Shaw 2015
[56] *On Isis and Osiris 12*

The highly acclaimed historian Joyce Tyldesley noted that the deities associated with the moon – Iah, Khonsu and Thoth – generally had a less "defined" mythology than those associated with the sun. The moon was generally seen as the sun's pale reflection and as such took a secondary role in many of the myths. Nevertheless, no matter what deity was associated with the moon, they were invariably also associated with timekeeping, the calendar, and administration in general, "a reflection, perhaps, of the role of the lunar temples in maintaining the monthly calendar," as Tyldesley puts it.[57]

When Thoth restored Horus's eye, he was essentially creating the moon. To the ancient Egyptians, the sun and moon were both "eyes," and depending on the religious center describing them, they belonged to the gods still. In the case of the moon, the eye was that of Horus, and, since it had been wrestled from its socket and damaged in the process, the moon waxed and waned in accordance with the violence inflicted upon it and its subsequent restoration. Just as the sunrise was a source of hope, so too was the waxing moon.

The moon was often associated with mystery, however, as was the knowledge associated with it and Thoth. There is a story written in Demotic during the Ptolemaic dynasty that appears to suggest the secrecy associated with Thoth's knowledge. It is called the "Tale of Setna-Khaemwaset and the Mummies," and it tells the story of a prince named Setna who, in his attempt to recover the "secret magic scroll of Thoth," comes across three ghosts, one of whom was the Prince Naneferkaptah. This prince tells Setna that he too once sought the secret knowledge of Thoth. He says he eventually found the scroll inside a chest at the bottom of a lake in Coptos, but, having discovered the knowledge, Thoth was furious. The god of knowledge sent a "slaughtering demon" to Earth that caused the prince, his wife, and child to all drown in the Nile. After that, the three were buried separately so that they would be estranged for eternity. Such brutality does not seem to be within the scope of Thoth's modus operandi, but it must be said that the earliest descriptions of Thoth do indeed suggest that he had a wicked temper and was not above dealing out destruction when he was crossed. Discovering the writings he deemed secret was evidently one of those crimes.

By the time of the New Kingdom, Thoth was credited with inventing the writing system that allowed Egyptian culture to flourish and span several millennia.[58] It was said that Thoth documented everything that happened each day and presented his writings to Re each morning. He and Seshat recorded the lives of humans, including their fates, as they were capable of seeing the past, present and future, and they both inscribed the length of a king's reign on the leaves of the ished tree too.[59]

Thoth's ability to manipulate the stylus is evident in the role he played in the Contendings of

[57] 2011
[58] Tyldesley 2011
[59] Pinch 2002

Horus and Seth, as well as that of his role in judging the dead. It also represented the physical manifestation of his vast wealth of knowledge. The writing system, as mentioned above, was one of holy symbols, not only because they tended to represent the gods and nature but because of the knowledge they recorded. It may be supposed, as is the tradition in Judaism, that the words Thoth used to ordain the universe with its immutable laws were written in the same hieroglyphs that decorated the tombs of the higher classes of Egyptian society.

The appearance of the Egyptian writing system in the archaeological record happened around the 32nd century BCE, predating even the Early Dynastic Period, which scholars agree started around the 31st century BCE. Thoth was also a pre-Dynastic god who most likely started as a simple moon deity,[60] but it wasn't until two dynasties later, in the first half of the 3rd millennium BCE, that Thoth's female counterpart began being worshipped. "Female counterpart" may seem like a dismissive title for such a laudable goddess as Seshat, but it serves as a useful purpose in this respect since she is variously referred to as Thoth's daughter and wife depending on the source. Also, there is very little doubt that Thoth was "lord." She was called the "Foremost in the Library," suggesting that she not only was a keeper of sacred knowledge but also the goddess of writing, timekeeping, arithmetic, and architecture. In this last respect Seshat was a very important figure. She was the goddess who measured the universe and under her name as "The Lady of Builders," she was the patroness of architecture, astronomy, and mathematics. She was depicted helping kings to lay the foundations of temples as early as the Second Dynasty, and she was in charge of similar projects in the divine "mansions" of the celestial realm. Thoth was, no doubt, the principal deity in these matters, but that Seshat was given such an array of characteristics – like Thoth – and that she features prominently in many texts, including the Book of the Dead, suggests that she was much more than the fulfillment of the Egyptian need for "duality" in their deities. She was an important goddess in her own right and capable of helping the highest classes of Egyptians realize her divine designs.

The class system is vital for understanding knowledge, and therefore the profound worship of Thoth in the ancient world. Literacy was reserved for the priestly class, and the tombs of "ordinary" Egyptians were not as elaborately "aided" by the spells present in the Coffin Texts until much later in Egyptian history. Furthermore, as suggested by the story of Prince Setna, there was an element of secrecy to the knowledge Thoth possessed, a common feature of ancient religions in general. The notion of secret knowledge was especially common to the mystery religions such as that of the later cult of Osiris and the Eleusinian Mysteries.

The tradition that stated Thoth wrote 42 books that included all of the knowledge for humanity would gain a lot of traction later on in Egypt's history. Later scholars believed that most of this knowledge was kept for adepts, but some of it was claimed to be preserved in the *Hermetica*, a body of work that purported to have been written by the composite Thoth-Hermes character "Thrice-Great Hermes" Hermes Trismegistus.

---

[60] Tyldesley 2011

The *Hermetica* is, as a collection of composite knowledge, a true testament to the cosmopolitan nature of Egypt during its time as a Roman province. It is a syncretic corpus more akin to a tapestry in which the strands of Egyptian, Greek, Roman, Aramaic and Jewish myths were interlaced to create a fascinating work of philosophy.[61] Like many of the works attributed to Thoth, the *Hermetica* generally included a dialogue between characters such as Thoth, Ascelepius, Hermes, and the Egyptian sage Imhotep.[62] Although the texts are generally considered to be "developments in Greek philosophy," most scholars today believe that much of what is contained within them was traditional wisdom and knowledge of Egyptian mythology that Egyptian priests had possessed for centuries.[63]

These texts later influenced early Judeo-Christian movements such as Gnosticism, whose adherents believed that a person could emancipate himself or herself from the material world through the acquisition and utilization of secret knowledge. Much later, during the Renaissance, people like Cosimo de' Medici became so fascinated by the recently-discovered Hermetic texts that he ordered famed translator Marsilio Ficino to cease translating Plato in order to make a translation of the *Corpus Hermetica* instead. It was the commonly held belief at the time that this corpus predated the Old Testament and its knowledge had a great influence on the budding occult and alchemical traditions sprouting across Europe at this time.

The Magician

Heka was the ancient Egyptian name for what a modern reader would consider "magic" today, and it was also one of the forces the creator used when building the universe.[64] Since in some cases Thoth was believed to have been this "creator," his name and the secretive power of *heka* were connected.[65]

Heka was less of an occult skill than a tough skill to achieve. It was not a power restricted to the gods or priests - ordinary people were capable of utilizing magic (or paying adepts to do so for them) in their daily lives to heal or protect themselves and others.[66] For this reason, in many of the ancient tales, it was the magician who was the hero, not the warrior.

This emphasis on magical skills is unsurprising since most of the religious functions in ancient Egypt were centered upon magical texts or spells that were used for everything from curing illnesses to protection in the dangerous land of the dead. Just as a sick child became Horus the Child and its mother Isis the Protector when a cure was administered, so too did those who performed magic become deities who were skilled in *Heka*, Thoth in particular. In this sense they would then "battle" the disease as a deity would have battled a malevolent supernatural force.

---

[61] Pinch 2002
[62] ibid.
[63] ibid.
[64] Pinch 2002
[65] Tyldesley 2011
[66] Pinch 2002

These myths were drawn upon in the same way that sympathetic magic draws upon an "equivalent" in order to define and transmute the supernatural forces in the world into a real-world solution for those in need.[67]

Today, the use of orthodox religion within a magical sphere, such as the syncretic use of Roman Catholicism in certain Caribbean religions, is generally looked upon with, at best, scorn and, at worst, violent indignation. However, to the ancient Egyptians, such separation of "religion" and "magic" simply was not a common practice. Geraldine Pinch referred readers to the illustrious editor of many of the early Egyptian magical texts, J.F. Borghouts, when the question of the "legitimacy" of myths in magical practices was raised. Borghouts said, "There is, however, not a shred of proof that a specific kind of 'unorthodox' mythology was especially coined à bout portant for this genre." Pinch goes on to agree with Borghouts by saying the efficacy of those magical spells that recalled myths would have been minimal-to-impossible if the patients were not familiar with them in the first place.

Just as the use of "good" and "healing" magic among the Cunning Folk of Britain was eventually stamped out, predominantly due to religious orthodoxy, so too was the knowledge of Egyptian *Heka* stamped out with the closing of the pagan temples in the 6th century CE.

The Messenger of the Gods

One of the reasons the Greeks equated Thoth with Hermes was his participation in certain myths as a messenger. Obviously, this was hardly the only role Thoth performed, but being a messenger was not the only role Hermes played in Greek mythology either.

In the case of Thoth, this role is most prominent in the myths in which he served the "reigning" monarch Re, the Solar God. Re's reign was defined by numerous rebellion attempts from humans and other gods.[68] According to the "Neith Cosmogony from Esna," Re learned that the serpent god of chaos, Apophis, was planning on rebelling against him. As a preemptive attack, Re sent Thoth "Lord of the Words of the God" to battle the beast. Having sent his representative, Re's mother took the form of the Ihet-Cow and, while cradling the young Solar God between her horns, swam to Sais in order to give Re time to grow strong and return to battle his enemies. Thoth emerged victorious and Re was able to return to his throne. Thus, another danger to Re was averted thanks to the heroic magician.[69]

In a myth from the Upper Kingdom city of Kom Ombo, a place that worshipped Sobek and Horus the Elder in particular, there was another rebellion, so Re, Horus the Elder, and Thoth all set off to Kom Ombo to find the conspirators. Once they had arrived, Re told Thoth to spy on his enemies, which Thoth did successfully, returning to the Solar God to tell him that he found no

---

[67] ibid.
[68] Shaw 2015
[69] ibid.

fewer than 257 enemies who were all standing around and "slandering the sun god."[70] This time it was not Thoth the Solar God sent to massacre these rebellious subjects but Horus the Elder after Thoth suggested he might successfully slaughter these men and their eight officers. It would seem Thoth was right since, as Shaw put it, "[Horus]…armed with all his weapons of war…slaughtered with such rage and violence that his face turned crimson from the blood."

After both gods and humans staged various rebellions against the aged Re, he decided that he was no longer going to continue ruling Egypt in person and woul dinstead depart from the land of humans forever. Being far removed from the Solar God was one punishment for the humans since Re's presence alone was considered a gift despite the rebellions. However, he also decided to punish them another way, as described earlier in Spell 175 of the "Book of the Dead." "O Thoth - so says Atum. You shall not witness wrongdoing, you shall not suffer it! Shorten their years, cut short their months, because they have done hidden damage to all that you have made. I have your palette, O Thoth, I bring your inkpot to you …"[71] Setting his affairs in order, Re installed Thoth as both the moon and his vizier in the royal court, and then left the mortal plane forever. It is unknown how many years the humans that predated this "mandate" were supposed to have lived, but this certainly seems to be one etiological story explaining human mortality.

In the story of Isis and the Seven Scorpions, Thoth delivers a message to Isis advising her that Seth has found out where she and baby Horus are, and he tells her where they can both be safe. Isis takes Thoth's advice and flees. As she flees, however, she takes with her the seven children of the scorpion goddess Serket (each a ferocious scorpion in its own right), who had vowed to protect her and her child from any apparent attack on them by Seth or his agents. As the cadre of fleeing deities traversed the country, they come across a rich house. The scorpions approach the house but quickly find that themselves being turned away by the rich woman who lived there. The disgruntled scorpions each removes his own stinger and passes it to the largest of the group, who crawls under the rich woman's door and stings her child. Suddenly the house erupts in flames, and not even a divinely inspired and a very sudden storm above can put them out. Isis appears at the house and, being kind-hearted, picks up the child and rubs its throat while reciting the names of each of the seven scorpions. When she does so, the flames abate and the storm ceases, such is the power of Isis' magical knowledge. Such magical knowledge was wielded by most of the gods, but, in the case of this myth, the destructive magic comes from an interesting mixture of a ferocious goddess' children and a fierce mother protecting her child, all orchestrated by the "message" from Thoth.

This is an excellent example of Thoth's role as a "messenger" god. Thoth was capable of acting of his own accord, but he was not above obeying the needs and wishes of Re when he believed them to be in keeping with the law of *maat*. Thoth's role is that of the "restorer of order," a role he embodied in many myths, most often by putting things back where they ought

---

[70] ibid.
[71] trans. Faulkner 2001

to be (like the Eye of Re).

Conclusion

There is a rare but important spell to be found in the Book of the Dead that encapsulates perfectly the role of Thoth as envisioned by those adepts who wrote it as far back as the 16th century BCE. It is called the "Book for the permanence of Osiris, giving breath to the Inert One in the presence of Thoth and repelling the enemy of Osiris." It is also referred to simply as Spell 182. The structure of the spell is in part a declaration of who Thoth is, spoken in the first person, and an oration to the great god Osiris "Foremost of Westerners" i.e. "Foremost of the Dead." The spell says, "I am Thoth the skilled scribe whose hands are pure, a possessor of purity, who drives away evil, who writes what is true, who detests falsehood, whose pen defends the Lord of All; master of the laws who interprets writings, whose words establish the Two Lands."[72]

Here Thoth's virtues are presented almost as if there were no other god that could rival his power or prestige except "the Lord of All," who is presumably Atum or Re or, most probably here, Osiris. The god "whose words establish the Two Lands" is a reference to the universal law that Thoth inscribed, but it is intended to strike a political note here also since the division between the Lower and Upper Kingdoms plagued Egypt for centuries. Whenever the two kingdoms were divided, there followed a period of brutal infighting and political turmoil, which must have been seen as contrary to the "words" inscribed by Thoth.

The Spell continues to refer to Thoth as the "Lord of Justice" and credits him with the talent for being "truly precise to the gods" and one who "judges a matter so that it may continue in being," clear references to Thoth's capacity for knowledge, fate, and the dependability of his skills for the rest of the gods and humans alike.

Thoth continues, "I am Thoth, the favoured of Re; Lord of strength who ennobles him who made him; great of magic in the Bark of Millions of Years [The Solar Boat]; master of laws who makes the Two Lands content; whose power protects her who bore him; who gets rid of noise and quells uproar; who does what Re in his shrine approves … I am Thoth who foretells the morrow and foresees the future, whose act cannot be brought to naught; who guides sky, earth and the Netherworld; who nourishes the sun-folk. I give breath to him who is in the secret places by means of the power which is on my mouth."[73]

The "power which is on my mouth" presumably refers to Thoth's magical ability, which is of such perfection that he appears to guard, guide and glorify the rest of the gods, Osiris above all. The spell continues with a declaration of obedience to Osiris, "Bull of the West," mixed with a reminder that it was Thoth who "made [him] flourishing for ever." The Scribe of Time also reminds Osiris that he "granted eternity as a protection for [Osiris'] members."

---

[72] Faulkner 2001
[73] ibid.

Thoth continues to declare the glories of this "Bull of the West" in this spell, calling on him to enact his greatness for eternity and praising him for "re-fashioning" mankind, presumably into a better version than that which rebelled against Re and was eventually destroyed by Re's Eye. "I am Thoth; I have pacified Horus, I have calmed the Rivals in their time of raging; I have come and have washed away the blood, I have calmed the tumult and have eliminated everything evil."

There is a connection between this myth and events that actually happened. In the 17th century BCE, an invading group from the Near East known as the "Hyksos" took control of the Nile Delta and set up a capital at Avaris in the north, where worship of Seth had especial prominence long before they arrived. The Hyksos recognized in Seth certain attributes of their own chief deity, Baal. Geraldine Pinch believes that this invasion not only cemented Seth's association with "foreignness," but also led to the introduction of the worship of foreign gods, such as Seth's Canaanite wives Astarte and Anat, in Egypt.[74] The Hyksos were eventually expelled from Egypt by southern worshippers of Horus, so this passage in the myth could well have been a memory of some such event that had since been converted into an elaborate myth and an established "fact" concerning the success of Thoth's arbitration.

The spell ends with a nod towards Thoth and Osiris's roles in the mythology of death. "I am Thoth; I have come today from Pe and Dep, I have conducted the oblations, I have given bread-offerings, as gifts to the spirits, I have guarded the elbow of Osiris whom I embalmed and I have sweetened his odour like a pleasant smell. I am Thoth; I have come today from Kheraha, I have knotted the cord and have put the ferry-boat in good order, I have fetched East and West, I am uplifted on my standard higher than any god in this my name of Him whose face is on high; I have opened those things which are good in this my name of Wepwawet; I have given praise and have made homage to Osiris Wennefer, who shall exist for ever and ever."[75]

Spell 182 closes, then, by giving the modern reader an insight into the funerary process, which priests would no doubt have had to follow according to the decrees of Thoth in his book, as well as the fact that it was Thoth himself who embalmed Osiris after the god was dismembered by his brother Seth. This kind of allusion to other myths is extremely common in surviving Egyptian texts, whose writers tended to assume that their readers – the educated elite – were familiar with the myths of their gods and goddesses. From the places Thoth mentions, there is a clear distinction being drawn between him and Osiris. Osiris, now dead, was mostly confined to the West, the Duat, the Land of the Dead, whereas Thoth was capable of traveling the length and breadth of the lands. He guarded the elbow of Osiris and the Solar Barque, and with his magic he bestowed order on the land and eternity to Osiris and his followers. In effect, Thoth is describing what he says explicitly in the final paragraph of the text, that he is "uplifted on his standard higher than any other god."

---

[74] ibid.
[75] ibid.

Of course, these texts were written by literate priests who believed that they wielded at least one aspect of Thoth's knowledge and power, so it is likely that they would splice their writings with homages to their "patron" deity, so to speak. However, there is very little in this spell that is not corroborated in other, often much older texts. That Thoth was a primal deity whose power seemed to be limitless except for the limits he placed upon himself in accordance with the immutable law of the universe and *maat* seems to be the definition of his attributes. As such, to reduce Thoth to the status of a mere "messenger god" or "the inventor of writing" would do a great disservice to the elaborate mythology that spanned over three millennia and would go on to inspire and excite the greatest minds of the Renaissance.

Ultimately, it has to be admitted that although Thoth may not ever have the recognition or prestige of other gods like Horus, Osiris, or even Anubis, whose fearsome appearance has stimulated the imagination of all who have ever feared death, Thoth's role in Egyptian religion either surpassed or supported those of all other deities.

Online Resources

Other books about Egypt by Charles River Editors

Other books about ancient history by Charles River Editors

Bibliography

Babbitt, F. C., (1936) *Plutarch's Moralia & On Isis and Osiris* Loeb Classical Library

Campbell, J. (2008) *The Hero With A Thousand Faces* University of Princeton

Frazer, J. G., (1922) *The Golden Bough* Macmillan

Graves, R., (1955) *The Greek Myths* Penguin

Griffiths, J. G., (1980) *The Origins of Osiris and his Cult* E. J. Brill

Kirk, G. S., 1996. *Myth: Its Meaning And Function In Ancient And Other Cultures* California

Mercer, S., (1952) *The Pyramid Texts* Longman's, Green & Co.

Meyer, M. W., (1987) *The Ancient Mysteries: A Sourcebook* Harper Collins

Oldfather, C. H., (1939) *Diodorus Siculus: The Library of History* Loeb Classical Library

Pinch, G., (2002) *Egyptian Mythology: A Guide to the Gods, Goddesses, and Traditions of Ancient Egypt* Oxford University Press

Plutarch. Plutarch's Lives. trans. Bernadotte Perrin. Cambridge, MA. Harvard University Press.

Shaw, G. J., (2015) *The Egyptian Myths: A Guide to the Ancient Gods and Legends* Thames & Hudson Ltd. London

Tyldesley, J., (2011) *The Penguin Book of Myths & Legends of Ancient Egypt* Penguin Books

Tyldesley, J., (2004) *Pyramids: The Real Story Behind Egypt's Most Ancient Monuments* Penguin Books

Wallis Budge, E. A. (1912) *Legends of the Gods: The Egyptian Texts* London

Free Books by Charles River Editors

We have brand new titles available for free most days of the week. To see which of our titles are currently free, click on this link.

Discounted Books by Charles River Editors

We have titles at a discount price of just 99 cents everyday. To see which of our titles are currently 99 cents, click on this link.

Printed in Dunstable, United Kingdom

67774093R00030